MY FIRST SIGHT WORDS AND SENTENCES

ACTIVITY BOOK

I am reading a book

I go to school in a bus.

This book belongs to

_____

Wonder House

a

Color the word.

at　　the
　　a

Highlight the word.

Trace the word.

a a a a a a a

a a a a a a a

Fill in the blanks with the word given above.

Anna is .... girl.

She has .... car.

Please get me .... cookie.

I live in .... big house.

2

Color the word.

at   am
a

Highlight the word.

Trace the word.

am am am am

am am am am

Fill in the blanks with the word given above.

I _____ a girl.

_____ I wrong?

I _____ going to school.

I _____ reading a book.

3

an

Color the word.

Trace the word.

an an an an an

an an an an an

Fill in the blanks with the word given above.

I have _____ idea.

Do you want _____ apple?

He met with _____ accident.

I need _____ envelope.

4

and

Color the word.

Highlight the word.

Trace the word.

and   and   and

and   and   and

Fill in the blanks with the word given above.

She _____ I are good friends.

He wants a bat _____ a hat.

I like to sing _____ dance.

I have a dog _____ a cat.

as

as
Color the word.

as   the
an
Highlight the word.

Trace the word.

as   as   as   as   as

as   as   as   as   as

Fill in the blanks with the word given above.

Do _____ I say.

He ran as quickly _____ he could.

I missed the test _____ I was absent.

I am _____ tall as you.

at

at
Color the word.

at and a
Highlight the word.

Trace the word.

at at at at at

at at at at at

Fill in the blanks with the word given above.

I hope we stay _____ that hotel.

Meet me _____ the coffee shop.

Look _____ the beautiful moon!

Don't look _____ the screen for too long.

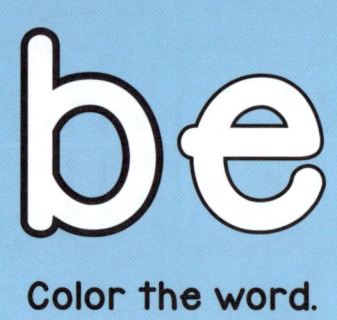

Color the word.

as   be
an

Highlight the word.

Trace the word.

be   be   be   be

be   be   be   be

Fill in the blanks with the word given above.

By when will you _____ here?

Don't _____ late.

I will _____ there on time.

_____ kind to everyone.

buy

Color the word.

Highlight the word.

Trace the word.

buy   buy   buy

buy   buy   buy

Fill in the blanks with the word given above.

I went there to _____ ice cream.

Do you want to _____ a new toy?

I can only _____ two shirts.

Did she _____ this sports car?

by

Color the word.

as   be

by

Highlight the word.

Trace the word.

by by by by by

by by by by by

Fill in the blanks with the word given above.

She sat _____ the pool.

He goes to school _____ bus.

She was scolded _____ her mother.

I sent the form _____ email.

can

Color the word.

can buy a

Highlight the word.

Trace the word.

<u>can   can   can</u>

<u>can   can   can</u>

Fill in the blanks with the word given above.

I _____ do it!

I _____ ride a bike.

That car _____ go really fast.

She _____ paint and read.

cut

Color the word.

as   be

cut

Highlight the word.

Trace the word.

cut   cut   cut

cut   cut   cut

Fill in the blanks with the word given above.

The grass needs to be _____ .

He _____ the cake with a knife.

She got a paper _____ .

I saw a huge tree being _____ down.

do

Color the word.

do   buy

a

Highlight the word.

Trace the word.

do   do   do   do   do   do   do   do

do   do   do   do   do   do   do   do

Fill in the blanks with the word given above.

_____ your homework.

Which one _____ you like?

_____ you know where she lives?

I like to _____ yoga.

far

far

Color the word.

far   be
cut

Highlight the word.

Trace the word.

far   far   far

far   far   far

Fill in the blanks with the word given above.

We are very _____ away from home.

Don't go too _____ to play.

My work has been fine so _____.

She is by _____ the best singer in our class.

Color the word.

fly   buy

a

Highlight the word.

Trace the word.

fly fly fly fly fly

fly fly fly fly fly

Fill in the blanks with the word given above.

Birds _____ in the sky.

Kids love to _____ paper planes.

He likes to _____ kites.

I wish I could _____ .

go

go
Color the word.

far   go
cut

Highlight the word.

Trace the word.

go go go go

go go go go

Fill in the blanks with the word given above.

I _____ to school in a car.

Don't _____ to the party.

You can _____ and ride the swing.

I _____ to the library daily.

got

got
Color the word.

fly   got
    a
Highlight the word.

Trace the word.

got got got got got

got got got got got

Fill in the blanks with the word given above.

I _____ a new comic today.

My parents _____ me a puppy.

You have _____ to be kidding me.

She _____ up early today.

has

Trace the word.

has has has has

has has has has

Fill in the blanks with the word given above.

She _____ some beautiful paintings.

He _____ gone out.

_____ she told you yet?

He _____ an interest in art.

he

Color the word.

fly   got
    he

Highlight the word.

Trace the word.

he   he   he   he

he   he   he   he

Fill in the blanks with the word given above.

_____ took my notebook.

_____ is two years old.

_____ has brown eyes.

Did _____ bring his toys?

her

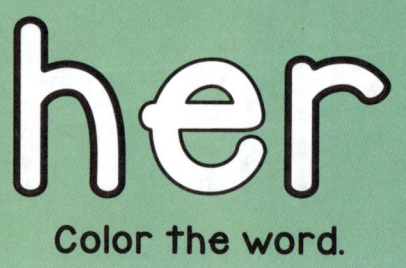

her

Color the word.

her   go

has

Highlight the word.

Trace the word.

her   her   her   her   her

her   her   her   her   her

Fill in the blanks with the word given above.

This is _____ house.

I am _____ friend.

This is _____ pet.

This toy belongs to _____.

hot

Trace the word.

hot hot hot hot

hot hot hot hot

Fill in the blanks with the word given above.

This soup is very _____.

Be careful! The pan is really _____.

It is too _____ to play outside.

Would you like some _____ curry too?

i

i

Color the word.

her   go

i

Highlight the word.

Trace the word.

Fill in the blanks with the word given above.

_____ like flowers.

May _____ help you?

_____ could read all day.

_____ like to play with my brother.

if

if

Color the word.

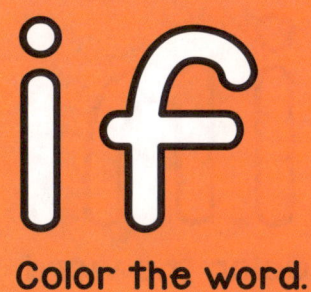

fly   hot
    if

Highlight the word.

Trace the word.

Fill in the blanks with the word given above.

_____ you are going to the market, can I join you?

I need to decide _____ I want a car or a puzzle.

What _____ James wants the same book?

Come back quickly _____ it gets cloudy.

Color the word.

her   go
      in

Highlight the word.

Trace the word.

in   in   in   in   in

in   in   in   in   in

Fill in the blanks with the word given above.

The horse is _____ the barn.

Please come _____ .

Put your toys _____ the box.

I like some sugar _____ my milk.

is

Trace the word.

is   is   is   is

is   is   is   is

Fill in the blanks with the word given above.

This _____ my book.

She _____ a smart girl.

What _____ wrong with you?

He _____ my best friend.

Color the word.

her   it
   in

Highlight the word.

Trace the word.

Fill in the blanks with the word given above.

Keep _____ on the table.

_____ is nice to be home.

Don't burn _____.

_____ rained today.

its

Trace the word.

its   its   its   its

its   its   its   its

Fill in the blanks with the word given above.

The doll has _____ own house.

The book is better than _____ cover.

The bird is in _____ nest.

The city has _____ own trains.

 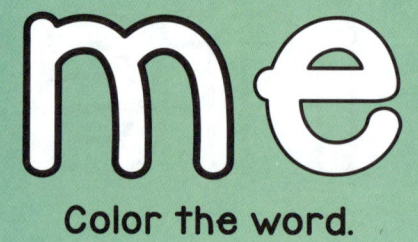

Color the word.

me   it

in

Highlight the word.

Trace the word.

me me me me

me me me me

Fill in the blanks with the word given above.

Please excuse _____.

Will you play with _____?

My friends love _____.

He is mad at _____.

 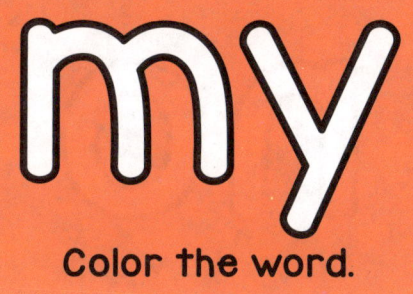

Color the word.

Trace the word.

my my my my my

my my my my my

Fill in the blanks with the word given above.

This is _____ house.

She is _____ mother.

Did you see _____ new shoes?

I forgot the ball in _____ room.

no

Color the word.

Trace the word.

no   no   no   no

no   no   no   no

Fill in the blanks with the word given above.

_____, he does not live here.

He pays _____ attention in class.

_____, I can't do that.

I had _____ idea about the surprise test.

30

Color the word.

Trace the word.

of   of   of   of

of   of   of   of

Fill in the blanks with the word given above.

She is part _____ our team.

Get out _____ bed.

Can I be _____ any help?

I am proud _____ you.

 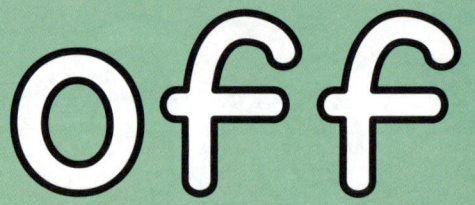

off

Color the word.

me   it
off

Highlight the word.

Trace the word.

off   off   off

off   off   off

Fill in the blanks with the word given above.

She took the day _____ .

Where are you _____ to?

_____ you go.

Turn _____ the TV.

32

on

on

Color the word.

my   its
on

Highlight the word.

Trace the word.

on   on   on   on

on   on   on   on

Fill in the blanks with the word given above.

The dog sleeps _____ the floor.

Don't spill water _____ the bed.

I am _____ my way home.

Write an essay _____ dogs.

or

Trace the word.

or   or   or   or

or   or   or   or

Fill in the blanks with the word given above.

Do you want to play _____ watch TV?

She wants a cat _____ a puppy.

Shall we go to the zoo _____ the mall?

He wants a red _____ white bike.

Color the word.

my   pull
on

Highlight the word.

Trace the word.

pull   pull   pull

pull   pull   pull

Fill in the blanks with the word given above.

Just give the door a _____.

Please _____ over your car.

Don't _____ my hair.

Can you _____ up the bucket?

put

Trace the word.

put   put   put

put   put   put

Fill in the blanks with the word given above.

_____ your book on the table.

She _____ on her coat and went out.

Where do you _____ up?

May I _____ the pot here?

36

say

Color the word.

my say
on

Highlight the word.

Trace the word.

say say say

say say say

Fill in the blanks with the word given above.

We should not _____ bad words.

Did she _____ anything to you?

Please _____ hello to him.

What did he _____?

sit

Color the word.

sit   it
off

Highlight the word.

Trace the word.

sit   sit   sit

sit   sit   sit

Fill in the blanks with the word given above.

Please _____ down.

Will you _____ with me?

Daisy likes to _____ near the tree.

You can _____ anywhere you like.

six

Color the word.

my   six
on

Highlight the word.

Trace the word.

six   six   six

six   six   six

Fill in the blanks with the word given above.

I got up at _____ in the morning.

Shall we meet for dinner at _____?

The train will leave sharp at _____ .

She has _____ dogs and one cat.

SO

Trace the word.

SO   SO   SO   SO

SO   SO   SO   SO

Fill in the blanks with the word given above.

I am _____ hungry.

Why did you come _____ late?

Thank you _____ much!

I love cake, _____ I bought two.

tell

tell
Color the word.

tell   six
on

Highlight the word.

Trace the word.

tell   tell   tell

tell   tell   tell

Fill in the blanks with the word given above.

What did you _____ her about the play?

_____ me a story about a penguin.

Do _____ us how the movie was.

Please _____ her to keep quiet.

41

ten

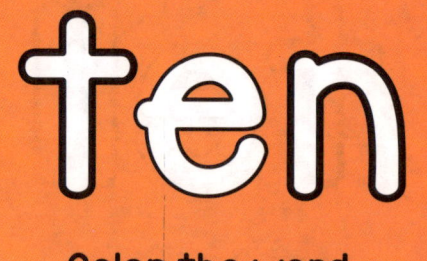

Color the word.

sit   so
ten

Highlight the word.

Trace the word.

ten   ten   ten

ten   ten   ten

Fill in the blanks with the word given above.

Let us meet at _____ outside the cafe.

My birthday is in _____ days.

I would like to have _____ glasses, please.

Will you be home by _____?

the

the

Color the word.

the   six

on

Highlight the word.

Trace the word.

the   the   the

the   the   the

Fill in the blanks with the word given above.

I went to .... zoo.

.... soup is too hot.

Can you pass .... salt?

.... postman is late.

to

Trace the word.

to   to   to   to

to   to   to   to

Fill in the blanks with the word given above.

I go _____ the park daily.

Give this book _____ him.

Don't go _____ the woods alone.

Let us go _____ school.

 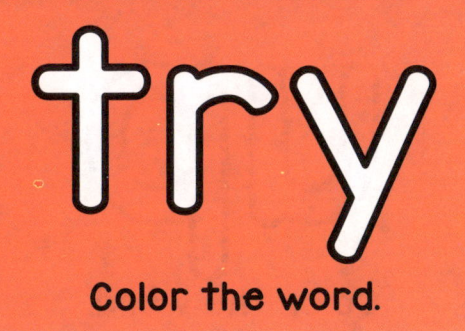

try

Color the word.

Trace the word.

try   try   try

try   try   try

Fill in the blanks with the word given above.

Please .... on this shirt for me?

.... this burger, you will love it!

.... calling the helpline.

Did you .... on the new coat?

Color the word.

sit up ten

Highlight the word.

Trace the word.

up up up up

up up up up

Fill in the blanks with the word given above.

I get _____ early in the morning.

I saw a plane _____ in the air.

Pull _____ a chair and sit with us.

Go and pick _____ another box.

46

us

US

Color the word.

the   try
    us

Highlight the word.

Trace the word.

US   US   US   US

US   US   US   US

Fill in the blanks with the word given above.

You can always trust _____.

Let _____ watch that movie.

His speech really moved _____.

Jasmine taught _____ how to dance.

47

use

use

Color the word.

sit up
use

Highlight the word.

Trace the word.

use   use   use

use   use   use

Fill in the blanks with the word given above.

Do you know how to _____ the computer?

_____ the right method at the right time.

_____ this money wisely.

Put your skills to good _____.

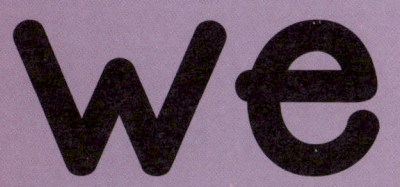 

Color the word.

the   try
we

Highlight the word.

Trace the word.

we   we   we   we

we   we   we   we

Fill in the blanks with the word given above.

_____ are best friends.

_____ go to the same school.

_____ might get late.

_____ are going to the mall.

why

why
Color the word.

why   up
use
Highlight the word.

Trace the word.

why   why   why

why   why   why

Fill in the blanks with the word given above.

_____ is the sky blue?

_____ is Leah crying?

Tell him _____ you will be late.

_____ didn't you open the door?

you

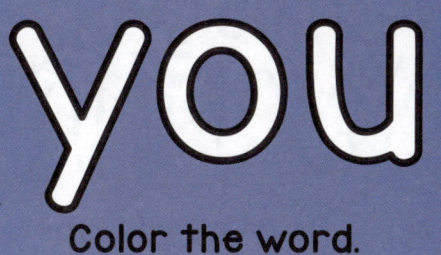

you

Color the word.

the you
we

Highlight the word.

Trace the word.

you you you

you you you

Fill in the blanks with the word given above.

Are _____ going to Paris?

_____ broke your promise!

I think _____ should study more.

Will _____ please shut the door?

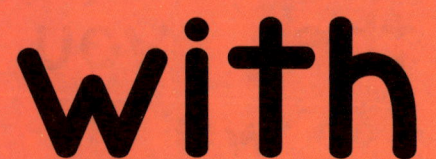

Color the word.

with   up
use

Highlight the word.

Trace the word.

with with with

with with with

Fill in the blanks with the word given above.

He likes to play _____ his brother.

Will you come _____ us?

Paint the picture _____ a brush.

She likes to eat bread _____ butter.